Happy 1st Birthday
Alex
From: Paolo

Cat and Alex and the Magic Flying Carpet

Cat and Alex and the Magic Flying Carpet

by Robin Ballard

HarperCollins*Publishers*

Library of Congress Cataloging-in-Publication Data
Ballard, Robin.
    Cat and Alex and the magic flying carpet / story and illustrations
by Robin Ballard.
        p.   cm.
    Summary: Alex's friend Cat recounts his adventures traveling
around the world on a magic flying carpet.
    ISBN 0-06-020389-7. — ISBN 0-06-020390-0 (lib. bdg.)
    [1. Magic—Fiction. 2. Carpets—Fiction. 3. Cats—Fiction.]
I. Title.
PZ7.B2125Cat   1991   90-33229
[E]—dc20   CIP
                                                                AC

To Mangy, Billy Tree, and Rabbit

One rainy day, Alex saw a strange thing.

It marched up the front steps and thumped
on the door.

"Hello, Alex," it said. "May I come in?"

Alex looked closer and saw his best friend,
Cat.

"Cat," said Alex, "you look cold. Come in
and sit by the fire."

Cat made himself snug in an armchair
while Alex brought him a cup of hot cocoa.
"That's a funny-looking thing you had on
your head," he said.

"That thing is a magic flying carpet," said
Cat.

"Where did you get it?" asked Alex. "Is it
really magic?"

"It was like this," said Cat. "Last summer, as I collected seashells at the beach, I found the carpet washed ashore.

"When the carpet was dry, I lay down on i
in the sun. The sun was so hot that I became
very thirsty. I reached out for my bowl of
water, but it wasn't there anymore. The carpet
had flown me to the Great Yellow Desert!

"The next day I lay on the carpet again.
This time it flew me to the heart of the jungle.

"My Grandmother Lion lives there. We played a game of cards and had tea with coconut cookies."

"Amazing!" said Alex. "Where else did you go?"

"Once I flew to a very big city,
where I spent the whole day shopping.

"And another time I flew to the top of the world. The wind was fresh on my fur, and my eyes saw all there was to see.

"But I missed my home, so I came back," said Cat.

Outside, the rain had stopped, and it was getting late.

Alex thought about Cat's adventures.

"I wish you could take me for a ride on the carpet," said Alex. "I have always wanted to go to the moon."

"We can go," said Cat. "Right now, if you like.
    "All we have to do is lie down and close...
our...eyes...."

Good night.